University of Nevada Las Vegas

In memory of Andrea Romero   1987-88

The Lighthouse Keeper's Daughter

by Arielle North Olson

Illustrated by Elaine Wentworth

Little, Brown and Company
Boston   Toronto

For my beloved Ole
— A.N.O.

For Ingeborg
— E.W.

First Edition

Library of Congress Cataloging-in-Publication Data
Olson, Arielle North.
    The lighthouse keeper's daughter.
    Summary: When her father's return to a Maine
lighthouse is delayed by a severe storm, Miranda
must keep the light going despite brutal weather
and her own illness.
    [1. Lighthouses—Fiction] I. Wentworth, Elaine,
ill. II. Title.
PZ7.051793Li 1987   [E]   86-20170
ISBN 0-316-65053-6

Designed by Trisha Hanlon

AHS
Published simultaneously in Canada
by Little, Brown & Company (Canada) Limited
Printed in the United States of America

The wind howled around Miranda's ears. She clutched the icy railing. One slip and she would fall to the rocks below.

She watched the raging waves for a sign of her father, but there was no boat in sight.

Should I go inside? she wondered. She inched her way along the slippery catwalk, but when she reached the door, she hesitated. If Father were here, he would scrape every bit of ice off the lighthouse windows, no matter how hard the wind blew.

Miranda could almost hear his voice: "What if there's a ship out there? What if the sailors can't see the light? There might be a shipwreck."

And now Father needs the light, Miranda thought, to guide him safely home.

She held onto the railing with one hand and braced her body against the fury of the storm. Then she began to scrape off the ice. Her fingers grew numb and her arms ached, but she didn't stop. When she finally circled back to the lighthouse door, she barely had the strength to open it.

Miranda stumbled inside the lamp room, and the wind slammed the door shut behind her. She pulled off her mittens and rubbed her icy fingers. Then she lit one of the big lamps. She warmed her hands by it and breathed in the pungent smell of whale oil.

How long had father been away? Two weeks? It seemed like years.

Miranda couldn't remember a stormier winter. For months, rough weather had kept the supply boat from making its regular stops at the lighthouse island. So Father had to brave the storm in their own boat.

"We're running out of food," he said before he left. "Keep the lamps burning tonight, and I'll be back tomorrow."

Did he reach shore safely, Miranda wondered, before the storm grew worse?

As soon as her fingers stopped aching, she worked her way around the circle of fourteen lamps, lighting them, one by one. They brightened the tower room and sent forth their warning to sailors at sea. BEWARE! ROCKY LEDGES BENEATH THE WAVES! LOW-LYING ISLAND AHEAD!

Miranda remembered how surprised she was last summer, the first time she saw the island. It was just a rock, miles and miles from shore. A huge gray rock, splashed by ocean waves. And perched on top were the lighthouse and a small stone cottage—their new home now that Father had become the keeper of the light.

As Father sailed the dory closer, Mother and Miranda could see that nothing grew on the rocky island. Not a tree. Not a bush. Not a flower.

Miranda could hardly believe it. She had packets of seeds in her skirt pocket, for bellflowers, sweet peas, and bouncing Bet. But where could she plant them?

Father lowered the sail and grabbed the oars. Then he rowed the boat in on the crest of a wave. It scraped bottom. Miranda's pet chickens fluttered and squawked in their crate. Father leaped onto the rocks and hauled the boat to safety.

Then Mother and Miranda stepped ashore.

"We'll unload the rest later," he said.

They avoided the pools and puddles by the water's edge and followed the rocky path to the top. A fresh sea breeze pulled at their clothes. Gulls called overhead, and puffins waddled about. The summer sun sparkled on the waves.

Miranda watched for bits of greenery along the path to the lighthouse, but there was nothing there, not even a blade of grass. When they left Grandma's farm that morning, pink roses had been in bloom . . . would this barren island ever seem like home?

"Look," said Father. "Here's an old coop for your chickens." It was made of odds and ends. Not fancy, Miranda thought, but it would keep the hens safe.

They climbed the stone steps to the cottage and pulled open the heavy door. Miranda walked quickly through the kitchen and peeked into the parlor. Then she ran upstairs to see her bedroom. It looked sunny and cheerful. She took an old cushion from the chair by the bed and put it on the wide stone windowsill. This is where I'll read, she decided, where I can look up and see the waves.

Then Miranda hurried downstairs. She could hardly wait to explore the lighthouse.

"Come along," said Father. "It's right through this door."

Mother and Miranda followed him from the kitchen into the storeroom at the base of the tower. Mother took just one look at the long circular stairs. "I think I'll stay down here," she said.

But Father and Miranda climbed upward until they reached the room at the top, with its circle of lamps and its windows all around. They looked out at the ocean. It surrounded them on all sides and stretched beyond, as far as the eye could see. Small boats dotted the water as fishermen and lobstermen went about their daily work. And far off on the horizon, a great sailing ship came into view.

Miranda felt wild and free, like the sea gulls that swooped and hovered outside the lighthouse windows. One landed on the catwalk railing and tipped its head to look at her. She laughed.

"Mother should have come up too."

"Do you remember what happened that day we were up on the cliffs?" Father asked.

Miranda nodded. Mother had almost fainted when Miranda called her to the edge to see a wildflower.

"It's strange," Father said. "Most things don't scare her, but she's always been afraid of heights."

Miranda looked down at the island on which the lighthouse was built. I like being up high, she thought. But suddenly her mood changed. The rocks below looked so bleak.

"Why doesn't anything grow out here?" she asked.

"In winter storms," Father said, "waves wash right across this island and scour it clean."

Miranda stared at him. "Then how can I have a garden?"

Father patted her shoulder. "Don't fret," he said. "Let's go down and fix that coop for your chickens."

Miranda wanted to look for Father's boat one more time, but now it was too dark outside. She checked the lamps again, replaced the glass chimneys, and started down the tower stairs.

Father wouldn't try to come back in weather like this, she told herself. Such heavy seas would swamp a small boat.

But he knows we are almost out of food. He'll be so worried, he might start out when he shouldn't. Miranda shook away the thought.

Surely he's at Grandma's now, waiting out the storm. He's probably sitting at her kitchen table eating apple pie. Miranda's mouth watered. For a week now, she and Mother had eaten just a bowl of cornmeal mush and one egg a day. But now the cornmeal was running low.

When Father came back from Grandma's farm, he would bring potatoes from the root cellar, pumpkins, nuts, and dried apples. Miranda felt homesick just thinking about it.

"Miranda."

She looked over the edge of the curving stairs and saw her mother standing on the floor below.

"Coming," she answered.

"You've been up there so long, I was getting worried." They walked back to the kitchen together, arm in arm.

It was suppertime, but it took only a moment to eat. Miranda wondered how long they could last on so little food. They pulled their chairs close to the warm stove, and Mother picked up her knitting. But then she put it down again and stared across the room. Miranda knew she was worrying about Father.

Suddenly Miranda realized how seldom she saw her mother's hands still. There were always socks to knit, shirts to sew, or trousers to mend. Soap and candles had to be made, the wood stove tended, and bread baked. Remembering the smell of fresh-baked bread made Miranda ache with hunger. She threaded a needle and darned one of her father's socks.

Mother picked up a book and began to read out loud, but her voice soon grew hoarse. It was hard to speak above the roar of the surf. She put the book away.

Each day Miranda watched for her father's boat, but the gale continued to blow. It was three weeks now since he had left. Miranda continued to tend the lamps the way he had taught her. She carefully shined the reflectors, cleaned the glass chimneys, and filled the lamps with oil. Then she trimmed the wicks and lit them.

More ice froze on the lighthouse windows. When Miranda stepped out on the catwalk, she was buffeted by the wind. A sudden blast of frigid air pressed her skirt against her legs and whipped off her scarf, tossing it out to sea. Miranda's teeth chattered. By the time she finished scraping, her hair was stiff with frozen spray. She hurried down to the kitchen to get warm.

"Miranda," cried her mother. "You'll catch your death of cold! Dry your hair!" she said, thrusting a towel into Miranda's hands. "I'll make some tea."

The next afternoon, Miranda was coughing as she made the long climb up to the lamp room. Snowflakes were swirling past the tower windows. Everything was gray and white—the sky, the sea, and the rock itself. A much heavier snow was falling.

It was so dark, Miranda lit the lamps early. Then she cupped her hands around her eyes and peered outside. Where was Father now?

The blizzard grew more violent during the night. Miranda had no trouble waking up to check the lamps. Her cold was worse, and the booming waves and the wind made it almost impossible to sleep.

By morning, huge waves began to wash onto the island. Miranda heard water slapping against the house. She looked out the kitchen window.

"My hens!" she cried. When the sea fell back for a moment, she raced out to the coop, with icy water swirling around her knees.

"Hurry!" Mother shouted.

Miranda caught all four chickens quickly and thrust them into her basket. Then she ran back to the house. Mother slammed the door behind Miranda just before the next wave broke.

Miranda dumped the squawking hens in a little storeroom behind the kitchen, then rushed back to the window. The chicken coop was tumbling in the waves. She pulled off her wet shoes and stockings and warmed her legs by the wood stove.

Giant breakers began to surge right across the island. And water was coming in beneath the kitchen door.

"Help me!" Mother called. They both knelt on the floor and jammed strips of cloth into the crack. Then they pushed heavy wooden boxes against it to hold the cloth in place.

All day long the blizzard howled around the cottage. Huge boulders were washed from one side of the lighthouse rock to the other, cracking and crashing as they went. The booming surf was deafening.

Miranda knew that the lighthouse at Minot's Ledge had been toppled by heavy seas several years before. She shivered. But ours is well built, she told herself. Father said so.

Miranda kept the lamps burning all day. And each time she climbed the lighthouse steps, her cold seemed worse.

By evening she felt weak and her fever was high.

"You're too sick to climb that tower!" Mother insisted.

"What if the lamps go out?" Miranda asked angrily. "Father said there was a lighthouse that stood dark for just one night, and two ships crashed against the rocks. No one made it to shore alive."

Miranda started up the stairs. Mother hurried after her. She steadied her daughter, and step by step they went all the way to the top. Then Mother sank down on the floor, scarcely able to believe how high she had climbed.

Mother and Miranda looked at each other for a moment. Then they began to laugh uncontrollably . . . exhausted and close to tears, but triumphant.

By morning,
Miranda knew the blizzard
was letting up. Even before she
opened her eyes, she knew. She could
tell from the sound of waves and wind. The ocean was never
still, but its wild roaring was somewhat muted now.

She snuggled down into her warm featherbed, remembering the
dream she'd had moments before. She had been walking through
Grandma's garden. Hollyhocks, roses, and poppies were in bloom, and
Father was coming down the path. . . .

Father! She bolted out of bed. She had to do his chores. Suddenly
she realized she wasn't dizzy anymore. Her legs were weak, but she didn't
feel feverish.

Miranda climbed the tower and snuffed out the flames in all fourteen lamps. Then she stepped out on the catwalk. Waves were no longer
surging across the island, and she could see no planks or broken masts
washed ashore. Despite the blizzard, the light must have been visible well
beyond the dangerous rocks.

Miranda went down to the kitchen and gratefully accepted a cup of tea from Mother. She didn't feel quite as hungry with the warm liquid inside.

"Father will be home soon," Miranda said.

Mother half smiled, but her eyes looked misty.

Miranda knew she was fearing the worst.

That very afternoon, Miranda thought she could see a dark speck on the ocean, moving their way. She ran down the tower stairs to the kitchen. "A boat's coming!"

Mother climbed the lighthouse with her, too excited to be afraid. They stared at the tiny spot until they could see it was a dory . . . a blue one . . . their own.

"It's Father!" Miranda shrieked. She ran down the stairs with Mother close behind. They threw on coats and slipped and slid down to the water's edge.

Father had to use all his strength to avoid crashing the boat on the rocks or tipping it over in the cold sea. They caught the rope he tossed to them. Then they struggled for footholds on the ice and pulled his dory in. Father jumped onto the rocks and gave Mother and Miranda a bear hug.

"Are you all right?" he asked. For the first time, Miranda saw tears in her father's eyes.

"We're fine," Miranda said. "Mother even climbed the tower stairs."

Father smiled. "You did?"

"I've been half mad with worry about you," Mother said.

"As was I." Father drew them close again. "I didn't know if I could get back before you starved."

"I kept the lamps burning every night!" said Miranda.

"That's my girl," he said. "I knew I could trust you . . . but I didn't know I would be asking this much."

They climbed up the icy path, loaded with bags of potatoes, chicken feed, and flour.

When they reached the kitchen, Father handed dried apples to Mother and Miranda so they could eat something right away — and Mother made a cup of hot tea for Father.

"You must be chilled to the bone."

"Aye," he said, "but happy."

He reached into an inner pocket and pulled out a book for Mother. Miranda could tell from the look on her face how much it meant to her. Mother gently kissed his cheek.

Then Father fished around until he found a small oilskin bag. He gave it to Miranda.

"Look inside. Grandma sent you something."

She untied the bag carefully and grinned when she saw what Father had brought to her.

"It's just enough dirt to start some seedlings," he said, "but I'll bring more. Your Grandma said there were gardens here years ago. Every spring fishermen brought dirt to the lighthouse keeper. The men would do it again if they knew you wanted it." He smiled at her. "I'll tell them how you tended the light."

Then he reached into his coat for small packets of flower seeds and gave them to Miranda. "Thought you might like these."

She read the handwritten labels out loud. "Columbine, larkspur, sweet William, candytuft, lupine, and Canterbury bells." She gave Father another hug.

"We'll have to see what grows best," said Mother. "I'll help you tend them."

By spring, the story about the girl who took care of the lighthouse had spread all along the Maine coast. Grateful seamen showed up almost every day with their gifts of rich, dark soil.

Miranda packed dirt into the cracks and crevices. She transplanted the seedlings, watered them every day and watched them grow. Soon there were flowers blooming all over the rock, in patches of blue, pink, white, and red. There was even a bed of lettuce a few steps from the kitchen door—enough for the family, and some for the chickens.

Boats sailed close to the lighthouse, just to see the gardens. Grandma came to see them, too.

When Miranda and Father worked in the lamp room, Mother sometimes climbed the stairs to help them. Together, they looked down at the brightly colored flowers. Could this be the same barren rock they saw last summer? The same rock that was battered by gales and high seas during the terrible winter storms?

Miranda knew they'd never let their supplies run low again. They would stay safe on their small island while the blizzards howled—and await the return of spring, when fishermen would replenish the gardens the ocean had swept away.

Author's Note

Parts of this story actually happened at lighthouses along the Maine coast.
At Matinicus Rock, a young girl kept the lamps burning for weeks while her
father was held ashore by the monstrous storms of the mid-1850s—and she
rushed into the waves to save her pet chickens from drowning. At Mount Desert
Rock, summer gardens were swept out to sea each year by winter storms.